I0457055

CHRISTMAS IN

Lululand

WENDY DEWAR HUGHES

Summer Bay Press

Summer Bay Press

Christmas in Lululand

Copyright 2017 © Wendy Dewar Hughes

www.wendydewarhughes.com

Published by Summer Bay Press
Editing, Interior Design and Cover Design:
Wendy Dewar Hughes, Summer Bay Press

ISBN: 978-1-927626-73-3

CHAPTER ONE

The snow had begun to fall by the time Elliott Robinson turned off the evening news. It came down in soft twirling flakes at first but before long lay in a thick carpet on the sidewalks and drifted heavily down through the glow of the streetlights. Before morning the wind picked up and had swirled all that fallen snow and more into drifts, which covered the front walk and formed crescents in the corners of the veranda of Elliott's house.

Elliott looked at the clock on the stove at 7:34 and decided that if he hurried he had exactly eleven minutes in which to sweep the porch steps and shovel the walk. He did not like to hurry but he zipped his parka, yanked the earflaps of his fur-lined hat down to his chin and pulled on his gloves. Outside, a blast of cold air hit him with stinging needles of snow as he grabbed the broom, which miraculously still stood in the corner behind a snow-filled flowerpot on the veranda. With the straw broom, its bristles worn down almost to the strings, he dispatched the snow piled on the steps, then switched to the snow shovel that he kept tucked behind the little spruce tree and flung the drifts from the walkway. It wouldn't do to go off to work having the house look like he'd let it go.

At exactly 7:45 Elliott locked his front door and set off. Five minutes later, he turned a key in the front door of Robinson's Hardware and let himself in. The bell over the door tinkled as he pushed the door closed against the bitter wind and went to turn off the alarm and switch on the lights. He could see his breath but once he edged up the thermostat, it would warm up. Elliott Robinson would never have described himself as parsimonious. He simply placed great importance on getting value for his money.

Forty-five minutes later, Ethel Martins blew through the store's door, setting the bell jangling again, and marched up to where Elliott stood behind the counter sorting bolts by size.

"Elliott," she snapped, "turn up that heat or I'm going to turn right around and go home. How do you expect a woman to work a computer when her fingers are frozen to the keyboard?"

Elliott stared at her for a full minute. He and Ethel had this disagreement nearly every morning. In winter it was about the heat; in summer it was the air conditioning.

"I've already cranked it up to sixty-five degrees," he said stiffly. He pushed his black-framed glasses up on his nose and studied how the wind had rearranged Ethel's mauve hair into drifts that resembled those on the sidewalks.

3

"If you won't turn it up, then I will!" she declared, and went straight to the thermostat and gave the lever a push. When she stomped into the back room to hang up her purse and coat, Elliott stepped to the wall and turned it back down, then calmly went back to sorting bolts.

Elliott placed the boxes of bolts in their slots on the shelf and pulled out several bins of washers. Why people couldn't put them back where they'd taken them from he didn't know. It irked him something fierce when things were out of place. He was about to set the bins on the counter when the front door burst open, setting the bell clanging and flying all the way back so it banged into a stack of neatly arranged cans of paint.

"Oh, my goodness," said a muffled voice as a woman in a bright pink coat reached for and pushed the door closed against the blast of winter wind. "A girl could get blown right off her feet out there today," she cried, brushing snow from the front of her coat with one hand. In the other hand she carried a heavy, black case. She wore tall black boots with heels so high that Elliott had to wonder how she could navigate on them even on days when the sun shone and the sidewalk was dry and smooth, much less on a day like today. The woman set her case on the floor, pulled off a pair of cobalt blue gloves and, spreading her fingers, ran her hands up into a mass of windblown, pale blonde curls. Giving her head a shake, she said, "That's better," then swept up the case and marched over to where Elliott stood, her hips swaying and those heels tapping on the linoleum tile floor.

"Good morning," she said, her deep pink lips curving into a wide smile. "Are you the manager?" She blinked her wide blue eyes and Elliott could see melted snow sparkling on her long, black lashes. He sucked in his stomach and straightened, pressing his shoulders back.

"I'm the owner of Robinson's, ma'am. How may I help you?"

She stuck out her hand with fingers that were tipped in long, bright pink nails with something sparkly on them and said, "My name is Lulu Davis. I'm the sales rep with Gifts Aplenty Agency. I represent eighteen different giftware lines. If you have a few minutes I can show you my catalogues and help you get some more merchandise in your store. I know the season is getting a little late but see by your windows that you must have already sold out of your Christmas stock so you'll want to order more right away before the real rush starts."

Elliott took her hand in his and she gave it a firm shake. He wasn't sure but he thought she even winked at him. She leaned over to where she had set her case by her feet and Elliott leaned, too.

She popped back upright, pushing a big looping curl from her eyes and slid the bins of washers out of the way. She dropped an armful of catalogues and

6

binders on the counter. "You haven't told me your name yet, honey," she said, leaning a little toward Elliott, just close enough so he could inhale her perfume. *Something musky and exotic*, he thought, but what would he know?

"I'm, uh, I'm Elliott, Elliott," he said, unsure why his mouth chose this moment to stop working properly. "Uh, Elliott Robinson." He waved a hand vaguely toward the front of the store to indicate the sign over the door. "Uh, I am sorry, miss, but I don't need any more stock for Christmas…" He trailed off, staring at how her eyebrows shot up into perfect crescents over her sparkling blue eyes. *How did a person ever get eyes that blue?* he wondered.

Lulu Davis turned around and surveyed the store, one hand on her hip and the other tapping the counter with those long nails. "Elliott, honey, I know you're putting me on. Look at those windows." She flung a hand in the direction of the display windows, one side decorated with three paint cans and the other with snow shovels and sacks of road salt. "How do you expect to get anyone in here to shop for Christmas when your front windows look like that?" She swung around and tilted her head to one side, gazing into Elliott's grey eyes. He cleared his throat and pushed up his glasses.

"Now, just have a look at this catalogue for five minutes and in only a few days you and I will have those front windows transformed into a holiday wonderland. Every woman in town is going to be in here buying toys for the children, gifts for daughters, sisters, and moms, and guy stuff for their men."

"But, but, they all usually go to the mall in Painesville," Elliott stuttered. "Nobody shops for Christmas here. "

Lulu laid a slender hand on Elliott's sweatered arm. "It's easy to see why, Elliott, honey, when there's nothing for them to buy." Her voice was soft with sympathy and she gazed into his eyes again and gave a long, slow blink.

An hour and a half later, Elliott Robinson had ordered more than three thousand dollars worth of giftware, Christmas decorations, toys, woollen scarves, men's boxed shirt and tie sets, jewellery boxes, bath products, and three fully flocked Christmas trees, complete with all the trimmings. When Ethel emerged from the back office to give the thermostat another push, Elliott informed her that he was going out for lunch with Miss Lulu Davis and would return in one hour.

Open-mouthed, Ethel watched Elliott don his coat and gloves and usher the big-haired, shapely, long-legged, bright-pink-lipped, eyelash-flapping woman out the door. In the entire forty-two years that she had known him, from the time he wore diapers, she had never seen him look like that. She saw him smooth down his dark brown curls, the only wild thing about him, as he closed the door and headed down the street toward Clayton's Café with Lulu Davis' hand tucked firmly in the crook of his arm.

Ethel's head wagged back and forth as Elliott disappeared from sight. Then she sniffed and muttered, "That woman has 'gold-digger' written all over her."

CHAPTER TWO

After struggling against the bitter wind that swept down Delamere's main street, Clayton's Café felt warm and welcoming to Lulu Davis. The scent of bacon and cinnamon buns and hot coffee drifted past her as Elliott steered her smoothly toward a booth near the back. She slid onto the red leatherette seat and plopped her leopard-print purse down beside her. She looked across the table at Elliott Robinson.

Lulu had met lots of men like Elliott in her going-on-five-years as a giftware sales rep. They owned mom and pop stores in little towns all over her territory. They were good, honest people for the most part but the orders they placed barely afforded her enough commission to live on. Not that she complained; she enjoyed life too much to waste any time griping about her lot, and she loved the gift business and the travel. But lately she had felt herself wanting something else—a real home and a family—before it was too late. At thirty-four, Lulu knew that time was running out if she ever hoped to hold a child of her own in her arms.

"You want menus, El?" a woman called from over the swinging half-doors that separated the kitchen from the rest of the café.

"Sure, Tammy," Elliott answered over his shoulder.

Lulu saw the woman give an exaggerated roll of her eyes before grabbing a couple of plastic-covered menus and slapping them down on the table. "Coffee?" she offered Lulu.

"No, thanks," Lulu answered, smiling big. "It makes me all jittery."

"Well," Tammy said, "we wouldn't want that now, would we? I'll be back in a minute to take your order. You want the same as always, El?"

Elliott nodded as Tammy strode back into the kitchen.

"You must come here all the time," Lulu said to Elliott, tilting her head.

"Everyday, almost."

"So tell me about your store," she prompted. "Have you owned it for long?"

Elliot pressed his wayward curls down against his head again. "My father left it to me. I've owned it since I was twenty-two years old. That was the year he died of a heart attack," Elliott explained as he twirled a fork in one hand. "Oddly enough, my grandfather died at the same age as my father did, forty-two."

"I'm so sorry," Lulu said, reaching across the table to squeeze Elliott's wrist briefly. "That must have been difficult for you."

Elliott shrugged. "It wasn't easy taking over the store that young," he said. "After mom passed away, I took over the house, too."

Lulu could see a flush start up Elliott's neck. She hated to see anyone uncomfortable and usually started talking as a diversion from further anxiety or embarrassment. Elliott Robinson was not a supremely handsome man but his face had a kind of sensitivity, like someone who had known pain. She could see it in his eyes. Lulu believed that you could tell a lot about someone from his eyes if you really looked. Sometimes she would study her customers, store owners or buyers, and just knew whether they would pay on time or if they were the type to make the company wait sixty, ninety, or even a hundred and twenty days to pay a net-thirty invoice. Looking at Elliott now, she knew he was not one of those.

"I never knew my father," she said. "My mom was only sixteen when she had me and he was long gone before then." She said it without remorse. It was an old story but it was her story. "She left not long after so I grew up with my grandmother. My own grandfather died when I was young and I was eight when Gran died. After that I went into foster care and saw my mom about once a year until I was fifteen. That's when I ran away, got a job, finished high school, went to college, got married for about five minutes and got divorced. The first time he blackened my eyes it was over, and well, here I am." She shrugged and spread her hands out, palms up.

Tammy showed up to take her order.

"That makes my life seem like a piece of cake," Elliott remarked. "And your mom named you Lulu?"

She laughed. "Goodness no! She named me Louetta-Louise Lootendorfer. She thought it was cute. Good grief, right? I changed it to Lulu the moment I could talk. The only good thing that skunk of a guy I married gave me was a last name that wasn't Lootendorfer."

Elliott laughed out loud. He hardly ever did that. When their food arrived, his order turned out to be a grilled ham and cheese sandwich on rye bread and a side salad with Italian dressing—the exact same thing that she had ordered.

"How freaky is that!" Lulu cried when Tammy set the plates down. Elliott just smiled.

A while later he pushed his empty plate away. "How long will you be in Delamere?"

"Well, I planned to be here only for the morning but it looks like fate had other plans. I hit a patch of black ice coming into town, spun around about three times and smacked into a light post. The guys at the garage told me it could take up to a week before they get the parts to fix my car so I guess I'm stuck. I'd catch the bus and go back to the city but there's nothing waiting for me there."

Elliott saw her shoulders sag. "I guess I'll just get a room at that little inn I saw up the road and consider this a surprise vacation. It's getting too late in the season for sales anyway. This was going to be my last trip until after the New Year when the gift shows start."

"There's not much to do in Delamere," he said, "especially when the weather's bad."

"Oh, you don't have to worry about me," she said, waving his concern away. "As long as there's a library, or even a drugstore with a spinner full of paperbacks I can occupy myself. Besides, I've already submitted all your orders and they should start arriving in a couple days. I can help you unpack and merchandise everything."

Her eyes sparkled as she proceeded to suggest all the ways they could decorate the store together. When it came time to pay the bill, Elliott slid a twenty across the table to Tammy to cover the $12.99 their lunches cost and told her to keep the change. Tammy's eyes bulged and her mouth dropped open but, with one severe look from Elliott, she backed away. He held out his hand to help Lulu to her feet, tucked her arm in against his side and led her out of the restaurant.

Tammy watched them go without moving until they were out of sight. Then she picked up the phone and punched in some numbers.

"Ethel," she said, "you're not going to believe what just happened to me. Elliot left me a seven-dollar tip."

"We're going to have to put a stop to whatever might be fixin' to go on," Ethel snapped, "before it has a chance to get started."

CHAPTER THREE

Tammy Carter tucked that seven-dollar tip into the pocket of her jeans and allowed herself a tiny smile. She had seen the look in Elliott's eyes as he gazed across the table at that blowsy blonde woman. She too wanted to nip in the bud any attraction that might be starting to simmer between those two.

Tammy and Elliott had known each other since they were children and had grown up together through all their school years in Delamere. She wasn't in love with him but as life-long friends, she thought they would make a good match. Since the love of her life had taken off a few years before with that woman from Painesville, Tammy had been scrambling just to get by. Her two children had finished high school and gone off to college but the bills never ended. Tammy knew from bits of information provided by Ethel, Robinson's Hardware's bookkeeper, that while Elliott may not like to *spend* money, that didn't mean he didn't *have* money.

A few weeks earlier, Tammy had slid into the booth opposite where Elliott sat having his lunch.

"Hey, El," she said, "I've been thinking."

"Oh?" Elliott answered through his grilled ham and cheese. She saw his brow furrow. Not a good sign. She decided she might as well jump in with both feet.

"We've known each other a long time, we're both single, and we're not getting any younger, either of us. Maybe you and I should, you know, think about our futures. Maybe we could have a future together..."

Elliott gulped and gagged a bit, as if he had forgotten to chew the bite of sandwich in his mouth. His eyes watered and he took a big swallow of water. "Are you suggesting we get married?" he asked when he had caught his breath.

"Uh, well yeah, maybe," Tammy stammered, "something like that."

Elliott reached across the table and took Tammy's hand in his. "That's a nice thought, Tam," he said, "but I don't think it would work. We're probably better off the way things are."

When he had finished his meal, she watched him leave the restaurant. "It might be better for you," she muttered, "but I doubt that it will be better for me." She pushed herself onto her sore feet and went back into the kitchen.

After a few days the snowstorm abated and the deliveries of Christmas stock for Robinson's

Hardware began to roll in. First to arrive was the shipment with three white trees for the window displays, complete with all the decorations, tinsel, lights, and dangly ornaments, each set with its own colour scheme.

Lulu called the garage every day to see if her car was ready and was first told that the part would be in the next day, then that the part was on back-order and would be another week. She considered hopping on the bus and heading home but she loved the quiet little inn with its cozy chairs by the fire, the hearty home-cooked breakfasts, and the downy duvet to cuddle under at night. She hadn't had a real vacation for a long time so she decided to make her stay in Delamere her vacation time. She didn't have to rush home to look after a pet and, honestly, she knew that no one would miss her if she never came home at all. Her landlady might start to wonder after a while but she had even left post-dated cheques for the rent for the next six months.

On the fourth day of her stay, she wrapped a thick scarf around her neck and ventured out. The wind had dropped but the clouds hung low like a bad attitude and threatened more snow any minute. Picking her way past icy patches, Lulu walked down Main Street, gazing into store windows and admiring the sparkling wreaths hanging on the charming streetlamps. When she arrived at Robinson's Hardware, all she saw in the windows were piles of boxes, most of them still taped closed. She pushed the door open and entered, the bell tinkling overhead. A few customers nosed around the premises and she could see Elliott behind the counter ringing up a purchase for a man in painters' whites. Within a few minutes the store was empty except for Lulu and Elliot. She approached with a smile.

"Hello again, Mr. Robinson," she said.

Elliott looked up. He seemed startled to see her.

"I notice that some of your stock has arrived already," Lulu said, not waiting for him to speak. "I can see that you're busy, and since I'm stuck in town waiting for car parts and with nothing to do, why don't I give you a hand unpacking and merchandising everything? I'm pretty good at window displays."

Elliott glanced at the boxes in the window and scattered on the floor in front of them. "I can't ask you to do that," he said.

"You're not asking," Lulu said. "I'm offering. Not the same thing. I was getting bored at the inn and it looks like I'll be here a while longer. Please give me something to do...unless you don't want me to."

He cast another glance at the boxes. "All right, I accept," he said, reaching under the counter and producing a knife to slash the packaging. "Have at it."

Over the next four hours, Lulu unpacked, priced, sorted and set up. First she assembled the white, flocked Christmas trees and placed the large one and the smallest one in one window and the medium-sized one in the other window. Next came the twinkling lights, followed by masses of decorations. The largest tree sported an ornate theme in shades of burgundy and gold; the small tree was dressed in emerald greens and midnight blues. For the tree in the other window, Lulu had suggested a playful theme with multi-coloured characters and baubles, which Elliott had agreed to order, and she now arranged.

Halfway through setting up the windows, the UPS truck arrived and disgorged another dozen boxes of stock. By the time daylight outside began to fade, Lulu was exhausted, but only partway through unpacking and pricing the new stock. With the trees lit, the few townspeople who had ventured out now stopped to admire the Christmas mirage that was taking shape in Robinson's windows.

Elliott too, had been watching the windows transform from a neglected wasteland into a imaginative wonderland and marvelled at Lulu's abilities to turn cardboard boxes full of stuff into such beautiful exhibits. Lulu sat down on the window shelf as Elliott approached.

"They look wonderful," he said, softly. "I could never have done what you have done here."

Ethel strode past yanking her winter coat over her shoulders and tugging on her gloves. "I could have," she said with a snort, "but I notice that you didn't ask me."

"You were too busy," Elliott said, giving her a quizzical look. She had never showed any interest in merchandising stock before in all the years she had worked in the store.

"Well," Ethel jerked open the front door, "you'll never know for sure now, will you? Not with Miss Fancy Lady here doing it for you." With that she slammed the door behind her and marched off down the street.

Elliott cast a sideways glance at Lulu who bit the inside of her bottom lip as she stared after Ethel. She looked back at Elliott and when their eyes met, they burst into laughter.

"I don't know what came over her," Elliott said. "She has never shown the slightest interest in decorating the store."

"'Miss Fancy Lady'?" Lulu said. "I don't think anyone has ever called me that before. I'm not sure whether to be insulted or flattered."

"Let's settle on 'flattered' and go for dinner. It's time to close up anyway."

They chose the Chinese restaurant on the corner and ordered ginger beef, lemon chicken, and fried rice, sitting across from one another in a tiny booth near the front window. Only one other couple shared the restaurant on the chilly evening. By now almost no one was out on the slippery streets and it had begun to snow again. Over tiny cups of green tea, Lulu and Elliott discovered that they both liked many of the same books, had similar tastes in politics, and each attended church on Sundays, singing in the choir.

"I love opera," Elliott said, "though I hardly ever get to go to a real one. It's hard to get away from the store, even for an evening."

"I love opera too," Lulu cried. "I have season's tickets. It's my big self-indulgent splurge. I buy two passes so that I can invite a friend but often I end up going alone anyway." Then her face lit up. "Why don't you come with me when the next one is on?"

"I have a good idea," Elliott said. "The college over in Painesville is performing the Rimsky-Korsakov opera called *Christmas Eve*. Have you ever seen it? If we go to the Sunday performance, the store will be closed."

"It's a date," Lulu agreed.

When Elliott offered to walk Lulu back to the inn, she considered refusing but the wind had picked up again outside and heavy snow slashed down the street at a sharp angle. Besides, she liked Elliott a lot and when he offered her his arm as they headed down the windswept sidewalk, she took it, snuggling close to him against the biting gusts.

At the inn's carved wooden door, they stopped beneath the glow of an old-fashioned coach lamp. "I had a great time this evening," Elliott said, taking Lulu's hands in his. "And you don't know how much I appreciate what you're doing with the store. I just hope the weather clears so that people will venture out to shop."

"Look at it this way," she replied. "If it doesn't clear, no one will be going off to the mall in Painesville. They'll want to shop locally and you'll be the only store in town."

He grinned. "It could work," he said. "Something is going to have to happen for me to sell all the stock before Christmas."

"Don't you worry, honey," Lulu replied. "Once I've finished dressing up the place, no one will be able to resist coming into your store. It will be like a Christmas wonderland." Then she put her two gloved hands on the sides of his face and kissed him. Before he realized what had happened, she'd opened the inn door and disappeared inside.

He stood on the veranda under the coach lamp and pressed his lips together, savouring the sensation of hers on his.

On the street, a car crept past and Tammy stared sideways out the drivers' side window. She could have sworn that she had just seen Elliott kissing that Lulu woman on the steps of The Coach Light Inn.

CHAPTER FOUR

Within a couple of days all the stock that Elliott had ordered under Lulu's coaching had arrived and she had spent happy hours unpacking and sorting the decorations, toys, glassware, jewellery and even a line of purses that Elliott had been skeptical about but Lulu had insisted would sell. "In fact, I'll buy the first one," she told him when she unwrapped them. "I've had my eye on this style all season but I can't get just one."

"Take it," he replied, to Ethel's astonishment. "Take anything you like. You're a marvel and worth every cent I'm paying you."

Lulu stopped sorting a line of key chains featuring dogs and cats and looked up at him. "You're not paying me," she said.

"Of course I will pay you," Elliott objected.

"No, you won't. I'm doing this because I love doing it, and because I'm stuck here until my car gets fixed. You're doing me a favour."

From her vantage point behind the counter, Ethel listened to and eyed the two of them. Then she slipped into the office and picked up the phone. Through the tinted glass separating the office from the retail floor she kept an eye on Elliott but he seemed in no hurry to leave Lulu alone.

"Tammy," she said into the phone, her voice barely above a whisper, "I think it's time to launch our strategy. I've been doing a little investigating and you're going to love what I've dug up."

Two days later, when Lulu had received and priced every one of Elliott's orders and had put the finishing touches on the displays, Ethel decided the time was right. With the heavy cloud cover, darkness came even earlier than it usually did for this time of year. At fifteen minutes before five, Ethel emerged from the back office and stopped next to Elliott at the counter where he tinkered with a faucet handle.

"I sure hope all that Christmas stock sells," she began. "There's an awful lot of it. What are you going to do if no one comes in to buy it?"

"It'll sell," Elliott said without looking up.

"I heard via the grapevine that our Miss Lulu has talked a lot of other stores into buying huge orders and they've been left with most of it to mark down after Christmas."

"Who told you that?" Elliott asked, frowning.

"Oh, I have my connections in the retail world," she replied. "I've been at this a long time."

Elliott wondered briefly if she meant at the business of retail or the business of snooping into other people's lives. While she was as reliable a bookkeeper as anyone could want, she had a fondness for meddling that set his teeth on edge.

"What else have you heard from your so-called connections?" he asked sharply.

Ethel looked coy and smiled at him as innocently as a Sunday School teacher. "Now that you ask, I heard that she was married before."

"So?"

This response wasn't what Ethel had been expecting but she took it in stride. "Something, shall we say, shady, went on, apparently."

"I know," Elliott replied, turning to face her. "Her husband was a thief and a petty criminal and he beat her, but only once. She left him after that one and only time. She told me all about it. Her mother ran off, leaving her with her grandparents to raise, then her grandfather died when she was just a little girl."

"Oh," Ethel said, pursing her lips as if they had a drawstring. Elliott read disappointment in her face. "Well," she said, drawing herself up, "I just thought you should know."

"Why?"

"She just might not be everything she seems, that's all. And I thought I ought to warn you."

"You can go home now," Elliott told her shortly, turning back to the faucet in his hand. "I'll lock up."

After Ethel had gone, stony-faced and silent, her nose wrinkled like she had encountered a bad smell, Elliott locked the door and did his rounds turning off the lights. He left the tree lights on and they glowed out into the street, sparkling off the swirling snow. The windows looked beautiful and customers had already begun trickling in, complimenting him on how nice it was to have such a gorgeous gift selection right here in Delamere this year. Sales on the new product lines were picking up, as were sales of the regular hardware stock. People who didn't usually shop in Robinson's came in because of the gift and Christmas lines and left with articles they normally bought elsewhere. As he flipped the cover from the alarm he wondered again what Ethel was thinking. He didn't like this nasty side of her and he wouldn't put up with it in his store or in his private relationships.

With his index finger poised to press in the alarm code, he realized that for the first time in his adult life, he might actually be in the start of a personal relationship, of the romantic kind. He had spent several evenings since Lulu came to town either sharing dinner with her or having short text conversations about books or opera or the bad weather. He had spoken with her every day and when she had been working in his store, he neglected other work so he could talk to her while she worked. He loved watching how her hands with their pink-polished nails gently arranged each article or ornament so it looked just right. She often set up an entire line of products then re-arranged all the pieces so that they were all displayed to the best advantage.

The day before, Elliott and Lulu had attended the matinee performance of *Christmas Eve* at the college as planned. There had been enough of a break in the weather for the roads to open and Elliott had driven the two of them in his immaculate, if not exactly new, pickup truck. Afterward, they went for dinner at a tiny Italian restaurant and when they returned to Delamere, they had spent nearly an hour getting chillier and chillier sitting in the truck and talking about everything from the soprano's high notes to what trees grew best in the local climate.

The conversation was so scintillating that neither realized the passage of time. Lulu had snuggled close to Elliott to stay warm and his arm came around her shoulders. With his face just inches from her tumble of hair, he found the scent of her perfume intoxicating like nothing he had ever experienced before. He closed his eyes and inhaled deeply, wanting the scent of her to fill him up.

After a minute or two he realized that she had asked him a question and when he opened his eyes he saw her face tilted up to his. Without thinking, he lowered his lips to hers and kissed her, first softly then more deeply. Finally, despite the heat they created with their growing passion, the winter temperatures had won out and they said goodnight.

Now Elliott stood poised to punch in the store's alarm code numbers, savouring the memory and tasting Lulu's sweetness again. His cell phone tinkled in his pocket. He pulled it out and saw Lulu's name on the display.

"Hey, Lu," he said.

"Hey, you too. Want to come over to the inn and watch a movie with me? They're showing Christmas oldies and it's surprise night. The invitation includes gooey cinnamon buns and hot chocolate. Will you come?"

Elliott couldn't think of any other place he'd rather be on a night like this, than in the circle of warmth that surrounded Lulu. Just the thought of sitting next to her on the big overstuffed sofa in the inn's lounge filled him with a warm glow. As he set the alarm and turned the key in the lock to secure the store, he suddenly realized something that shocked him to the core. He was falling in love with Lulu Davis.

On the other side of town, Tammy sat across the kitchen table from Ethel in Tammy's little house behind the Big Bubble Laundromat.

"I tried, Tammy," Ethel explained. "He already knew and he wasn't fazed a bit. It's like he didn't care if she was something the cat dragged in after a night of carousing. We're going to have to move on to Step Two since Step One didn't have the desired effect."

"Okay," said Tammy. "I'm going to have to go through my closet and see what I can find. And with this weather, it's not easy to look desirable when you're wearing a parka and mukluks. "

"Invite him over for supper, silly," Ethel coached. "Elliott's too polite to turn you down. "

"I guess I could…" Tammy said. "And I have that little red dress I got for the restaurant Christmas party last year. "

"Do you want to live here the rest of your life?" Ethel asked, raising a pointed eyebrow as she glanced around Tammy's tiny kitchen.

Tammy sighed. "Not on your life. "

CHAPTER FIVE

Just when it looked like the weather would break and the sun might come out again, another Arctic front slashed down from the north bringing more snow, colder temperatures and fierce winds. Weather advisories warned everyone not to travel, followed by road closures due to blizzard conditions. The highway to Painesville closed to all traffic save the snowploughs and even they ceased to run when visibility dropped to zero. Then the power went out. High winds coupled with heavy snow downed trees and felled lines.

Robinson's Hardware kept the lights on and the heat high because, while the rest of the town shivered in the dark, Robinson's had its own generator. Elliott wanted it toasty warm so Lulu wouldn't catch a chill. Not only that but earlier in the fall Elliott had put in a supply of generators that turned his store rooms and basement into a series of tunnels through boxes containing power generators of every size.

People swarmed the store, leaving their cars and pickup trucks idling at the curb to keep them from freezing up, and loaded up with generators, plumbing supplies, electrical wiring and, since they couldn't go anywhere else to shop for Christmas, gifts for the entire family. The jewellery and purses that Ethel had sneered at, and had caused Elliott to question his sanity, sold out in a few days. The decorated Christmas trees went from being thick with garlands and ornaments to having to be re-arranged repeatedly to fill in the empty spaces.

Lulu fought the wind and snow every day and walked the three blocks from the inn to Robinson's. She told Elliott that she needed something to do besides sit by the fire and read and told herself that she was just going to help out her new friend in his time of need. Then she told herself that she went to the store daily so that she could be around other people. Eventually, she admitted to herself that it was Elliott she wanted to be with and didn't mind if no one else came within shouting distance. In fact, while she was thrilled at Elliott's success with the products she had sold him, she would have been happier if the two of them could have just been alone together.

With the power down, Tammy's scheme to invite Elliott for an intimate candlelight dinner at her house went right down the drain. Or it would have, had her pipes not been frozen. She had no generator and no money to buy one. Ethel, however, did have one. She had used her staff discount to put one in a few years earlier so her house still had heat and running water. For the duration, until the power lines were repaired, Tammy moved into Ethel's spare bedroom.

"This isn't looking good," Tammy complained one night after sharing a store-bought frozen pizza with Ethel while they watched re-runs of Magnum PI on television. "Elliott hardly ever comes into the cafe nowadays because he's so busy at the store. I don't know what he's eating for lunch. " She wiped her fingers on a piece of paper towel.

"Floozy-Lu has been bringing him sandwiches and treats from The Coach Light Inn every day," replied Ethel, rolling her eyes. "We're going to have to enact Step Three now, otherwise we might be too late. Elliott looks like a sick calf half the time. Lulu has wrapped him right around her painted-up little pinkie finger. If she comes on the scene for good, my retirement bonus might fly right out the window. After forty-three years at that store, I'm not letting anything get in my way. Fortunately for us, the opportunity dropped in my lap this afternoon."

The following day when Lulu arrived at Robinson's to re-organize the displays again, Ethel caught her attention and called her over with a flick of her finger. Elliott had gone to the basement to haul up more generators.

"I hate to be the one to mention this to you, sweetie," Ethel began, speaking barely above a whisper, "but I thought you ought to know."

Lulu frowned. "Know what?"

"The clinic called this morning with results of Elliott's tests." Ethel glanced left and right to make sure no one stood close enough to hear her. "It doesn't sound good."

"What kind of tests?" Lulu wanted to know, trying to remember if Elliott had mentioned having health problems of any kind. She came up blank.

"Well, you know that Elliott's father, God rest his soul, passed away when Elliott was just a young man. He had a congenital heart defect. He died in his early forties and so did *his* father. Seems it runs in the family." She sighed and placed a quivering hand on her chest.

Lulu gasped. "Is this serious?"

Ethel shrugged. "I guess time will tell but I suppose he could go any time." She reached out and patted Lulu on the arm. "I'm sure it's nothing you'll need to worry about though," she said and wandered back into her office.

At lunchtime, Lulu told Elliott she had to go check on the progress of her car repairs since the long-awaited part had finally made it through the weather. After receiving the news that her car would be ready to drive the next day, she stopped in at Clayton's Café.

"Hi Lulu," Tammy said, sliding a menu onto the table. "Can I pour you some coffee?"

Lulu glanced up at her and nodded. The waitress wore a look of gloom as she sloshed coffee into the mug. "What's wrong?" Lulu asked, genuinely concerned.

"Oh, nothing really…well, I suppose I can tell you." She slid into the booth opposite Lulu. "I had some bad news today. Apparently, Elliott's health isn't very good. I think it's something to do with his heart. His dad died young, you know."

"Yes, I heard," Lulu replied, now becoming troubled. *Could Elliott really be dying?* she wondered.

"Well," Tammy said with a sigh, "I guess there's not much they can do about it. Seems it runs in the family. What can I get for you?"

Lulu glanced at the unopened menu lying on the table. Suddenly, she didn't feel very hungry. "Just the coffee," she said.

CHAPTER SIX

As promised, Lulu's car was ready to pick up at 8:30 the next morning. She paid the bill with her credit card and slid behind the steering wheel, thankful that the car had been indoors all night. After stopping back at The Coach Light Inn and checking out, she pulled the car out onto Main Street. As much as it pained her, she knew what she had to do.

The bell tinkled over the door as she stepped inside Robinson's Hardware for the last time. She had really grown to love this place. By now most of the Christmas gift stock had been sold and the decorations had grown sparse on the once-loaded trees in the windows. Lulu gazed fondly at the displays she had created that now appeared well picked-over. She loved setting up the exhibits and realized that she had a real flare for it. *Well*, she thought, *that doesn't matter much now.* She knew she couldn't stay, couldn't get in any deeper with a man who might die before, well, before they even had a chance to get to know each other better. Before she could make her special Christmas pudding for him, before they could travel together or even have a family. She sighed. Who was she to think any of that would have ever happened anyway?

She found Elliott at the rear of the store grinding a key. "My car repairs are done," she said when he looked up. "I'm about to hit the road. I just wanted to stop and say good-bye." She knew that she was talking too fast but if she didn't get the words out quickly, she might start to cry. "I had fun working on the windows." She stuck out her hand for him to shake.

Elliott just looked at her outstretched hand as though she had just said something to him in a foreign language. He frowned, perplexed. "You're going home?"

Lulu nodded then dropped her hand.

"Aren't you staying for Christmas?" he asked. "I thought we could go skating together in the park once the wind drops. You haven't even seen my house. I took home decorations from the store and did it up really nice. I've never done that before…" He glanced at the key in his hand. "I was making a key to the store for you."

"I'm sorry, Elliott. I know we've had some fun times together." She glanced away, up an aisle toward the front door where her decorations had hung. A lump formed in her throat and threatened to choke her if she didn't leave soon. "But I have to go, get home, you know." She leaned toward him and kissed his cheek and felt something deep in her chest crack and break into pieces. Then she turned, ran down that aisle, and flew out the front door. Elliott watched her go, simply stunned.

Two days later, after fiddling with a light socket for about an hour longer than it required, Elliott put the socket back in its bin and went to get his coat and hat. He didn't feel like working at all and Ethel could look after the front while he went home for a while to lie down. Before he reached the coat hook, Max Parmin, a local contractor, strode up to the counter and thumped a couple of boxes of nails down.

"How ya doin', Elliott?" Max asked, examining Elliott's face.

Elliott looked up at Max who stood a good half a head taller and said, "Okay. Why?"

"You know, that thing with your ticker." Max struck his own barrel chest with his fist. "I heard it's not so sound. "

"What are you talking about?"

"I was over at Clayton's yesterday and I overheard Tammy talking to Ethel," he indicated the back office with a tilt of his chin. "I wasn't snooping, mind you. I just couldn't help but hear Ethel tell Tammy that the condition of your heart was pretty bad. Is it the same thing that your dad had?"

"What?" Elliott still couldn't fathom what Max could possibly be talking about. He knew there wasn't a thing wrong with his heart and told Max so.

"Well, I'm glad to hear it," Max said, paying for the nails. As Elliott watched him leave the store, something began to dawn on him. He stepped behind the partition and into the back office where Ethel sat staring at her computer screen.

Leaning against the doorframe, he said, "Did you tell Tammy I have a heart condition?"

"I don't know what you mean," she replied absently.

"I think you do. Look at me." Ethel dragged her gaze away from the screen and reluctantly looked at Elliott. "Did you tell Tammy that I have a bad heart?"

"I might have said something about that possibility. You did have tests recently, didn't you?"

Elliott didn't answer her question. "Did you tell Lulu that I have a bad heart?" He could feel the heat rising up his neck and suddenly knew exactly what had happened. Without waiting for his employee to answer, he grabbed his coat, hat, and keys. "Look after the store while I'm gone," he growled. "I don't know when I'll be back."

It was evening by the time he reached the outskirts of the city and while there had been a bit of drifting snow, once the sun went down and the wind with it, the roads were bare and dry. Now the stars sparkled in the cold night sky like flecks of crystal on black velvet. Elliott found the street overhung with leafless trees festooned with twinkling lights where Lulu had a suite at the back of a grand old house. He parked at the curb and jumped out of his truck, slamming the door behind him.

Jogging around to the back, he yanked off his glove and jabbed the doorbell button. The lights were on in the suite but he heard nothing in response, so he pressed the button again. This time he heard a muffled voice say, "All right, I'm coming." His heart leapt.

Light spilled onto the snow outside as Lulu pulled open the door. She had one hand clutching a fuzzy bathrobe up to her chin.

"Hello, Lulu," Elliott said.

"Elliott," Lulu said softly. "What are you doing here?"

He looked around, first up at the Christmas lights strung across the top of the door then at the tiny evergreen in a pot next to the wall, also decorated like something from a magazine. "I came…for you," he said finally, looking straight into her eyes.

"You'd better come in," Lulu said, reaching for his sleeve and drawing him into the warm room. "It's freezing out there."

Once she had closed the door firmly behind him, she stepped away from him and wrapped her arms around her middle. "Please tell me again why you're here."

"I came for you," he said, reaching out and lifting a wild curl away from her cheek. "Since you left, I've been useless. I can't think about anything but you. I can't eat, I put stuff away in the wrong places. I've even priced things wrong. And I'm babbling…" He shoved his hands in his pockets.

"I don't know what to say, Elliott," Lulu confessed. "I've been the very same but," tears sprang to her eyes and she flicked them away with her fingertips, "I don't think I can be with you. I don't think I could bear to lose you."

"Oh, for crying out loud," Elliott said so loudly that Lulu jumped. "Did Ethel tell you that I'm going to die young? Did she tell you that I have some heart condition that's going to kill me any day now?"

Shocked at his outburst, Lulu nodded. "I'm not sure I could stand to lose you, since I've only just found you. You're the first man I've ever really loved, I mean, *really* loved. The thought of losing you is just too much. "

Elliott reached out and folded her into his arms. "Lulu, my love, there is absolutely nothing wrong with my heart, except that you've stolen it. "

"But," Lulu looked up into his eyes, "Ethel and Tammy both said…"

"I'll deal with them later." His lips met hers and Lulu leaned into his embrace. After several long, love-sweet kisses, Elliott stepped away. "Do you mind if I take my coat off? It's getting hot in here and I have something I need to ask you. "

Lulu hung up his coat and then he guided her to the sofa. She lowered herself to the leather cushions. Dropping to his knee before her he said, "I know we haven't known each other long but I love you. I want you to marry me, to attend all the opera season performances with me, skate in the park with me in winter, and have a family with me. Will you, Lulu? Will you marry me?"

The tenderness in his eyes was almost her undoing, and with tears trickling down her cheeks, she nodded. "Yes, Elliott, I will marry you. I want all those things that you want. And I want them now."

Elliott could barely contain his joy. "How soon can we get married?"

"Well," Lulu answered, "the day after tomorrow is Christmas Eve. How about then?"

"It's a date," Elliott replied, and he kissed her again.

On Christmas Eve, the sun blazed across the sparkling drifts of pristine snow around the little church in Delamere. Elliott and Lulu had spent the previous day shopping for rings; then he had gone back home to arrange with the pastor for the ceremony and with the café for a little reception in their private room in the back. Lulu had shopped for a wedding dress, veil, shoes, flowers, and some new outfits for her wedding night and honeymoon.

It seemed like half of Delamere had shown up for the ceremony since everyone in town had known Elliott all his life. Only a few of Lulu's friends from the city had been able to come out but she didn't care. It was Christmas Eve and she was marrying the love of her life.

As the organist began to play, two figures in the back pew whispered to each other behind cupped hands.

"There goes my pension," Ethel moaned softly, gazing at Elliott standing up at the front of the church in his new tuxedo.

"Yeah, and it looks like I'm going to have to live with that miserable plumbing for the rest of my days," Tammy griped.

Ethel looked at her. "Why don't you just move into my house? It's too big for me alone anyway, and it will cost you a whole lot less. And my heat never goes off."

Tammy turned toward her and thought for a moment. "Okay, I will."

Just then the pastor asked the entire congregation to rise as Lulu appeared at the doorway wearing champagne satin scattered with sparkling crystals and began her slow walk up the aisle towards Elliott.

Tammy leaned over to whisper in Ethel's ear. "It looks like we're going to have Christmas in Lululand from now on, like it or not."

OTHER BOOKS BY WENDY DEWAR HUGHES
Available on Amazon and online book retailers.

Available in Print
and E-book

Available in Print
and E-book

Available in Print
and E-book

Available in Print
and E-book

Available in E-book Only

Available in Print
and E-book

Available in Print

Available in Print
and E-book

Available in Print
and E-book

Available in Print

Available in Print

www.ingramcontent.com/pod-product-compliance
Lightning Source LLC
Chambersburg PA
CBHW020340130626
46549CB00003B/1227